HOLD ME AT
Twilight

HOLD ME AT

Twilight

A Romano Family romance

Lucinda Whitney

Lange House Press

Edited by Michele Holmes and Ellie Mockett Whitney
Cover design ©2017 Lange House Press
Layout and Formatting by LJP Creative
Published by Lange House Press

First Printing April 2017

ISBN-10: 1-944137-24-6
ISBN-13: 978-1-944137-24-3

A pior coisa que ter uma família grande
é não ter família nenhuma.

The only thing worse than a big family
is having none at all.

Romano Family

- Francisco
  Mariana
  - Tiago
  - Catarina
  - Daniel
  - André

- Luís
  Glória
  - Matias

- Carlos
  Celestina
  - Jacinta

António
Teresa

- Manuel
  Antónia
  - Filipe
  - Luciana
  - Paulo
  - Ricardo

- Pedro
  Adelina
  - Gabriela
  - Juliana
  - Alexandre

- José
  Patrícia
  - Nuno
  - Susana

- Vicente
  Ana Maria
  - Carlos
  - Pedro
  - Dinis
  - Anita

CHAPTER ONE

*K*nox shifted his backpack and straightened. This had to be the place. Only one person occupied the store front across the street, a young woman with brown hair. He checked his information, confirming the address and the name of the business. Even if the regular agent wasn't in today, he still had to take care of the issue. After the day he'd had, he was ready for a good meal and a long night's rest. But even that was out of his reach until he filed a police report.

The travel agency nestled in a small space decorated with brightly colored posters of local popular attractions, and the window was dressed with gold letters and a garland of clear mini lights along the casing. His one-week business trip to Porto, Portugal, had kept him busy during the first few days, leaving no time for sightseeing. But the training had gone well, and he'd found himself with free afternoons

1

and evenings on the last three days, and out of ideas of what to do and how to use his time wisely.

After asking around, one of the Portuguese guys he'd worked with had recommended a local travel agency. Knox sent an email requesting ideas and the helpful agent had given him suggestions for events, trips, and points of interest. She'd also helped him figure out the train and bus schedules inside the city.

On impulse, at the end of the first sight-seeing day, he'd emailed her back to thank her, remarking on what he'd done that day. She'd replied the next morning with tips and more places to visit. They repeated the exchange for the next few days and he'd thanked her for making his time more enjoyable during his stay in Porto.

Several times she'd offered to help with anything else he might need, and he was just about to put that offer to the test.

When the light turned green, he joined the other pedestrians and crossed the street. Two older women chatted in front of the store window and when he paused by the door, they stopped and eyed him for a moment. Knox went in.

The young woman stood from her desk and said something in Portuguese.

Not again. Knox raised his shoulders. "I'm sorry, but I only speak English."

"That won't be a problem. What can I help you with?"

A temporary rush of relief came over him. Her friendly voice and ability to communicate filled him with gratitude. He felt the absurd desire to hug her but wisely resisted.

She glanced at the wall behind him.

Knox turned to find an ornamental clock with folk paintings of Portuguese icons. "You probably have an appointment and here I am barging in. I'll try to be brief."

She came around the desk. "No, I don't have any more appointments today, but we'll be closing soon."

The two older women who'd been on the sidewalk entered the agency and the woman's smile faltered. She said something to them in a very fast cadence, and they waved her off and sat on the two chairs along the wall. What was that about? Did she know them?

Knox turned back to the agent. "I had a J. Romano help me earlier in the week." He paused. This was turning more awkward than he'd anticipated. "Something came up and I could use some help today."

"I'm J. Romano. Are you a client of ours?"

It was her then. The woman before him with striking brown eyes and gorgeous dark hair also went out of her way to help others. His heart felt lighter. She'd made his trip so much more enjoyable. Well, up until last night, but that was completely unrelated.

He stepped forward. "Yes, I'm Knox Campbell. We exchanged emails this week."

Her eyes widened. "You're Mr. Campbell?"

"In the flesh." He grinned at her.

"I wasn't expecting someone so—" She studied him briefly, but recovered quickly. "I'm sorry. I'm being extremely rude. What can I do for you, Mr. Campbell?" Her expression softened in a gentle smile.

Knox hesitated. Someone so what? What had she been about to say?

"Did you extend your trip?" She asked, before he got a chance to reply. "I seem to remember that you were leaving today."

He'd be home by now if he'd left as planned. Maybe not that far, but at least closer to landing in New Jersey. "Well, about that." He blew out a breath. "Someone stole my wallet last night."

She gasped. The women on the chairs asked her something and she replied to them quickly. When they started talking in excited tones, she shushed them.

She turned back to him. "I'm sorry. You were saying your wallet got stolen? How awful." Her face was very expressive, her eyes full of sympathy for his situation.

Knox's ears heated. If it had been only his wallet. "My wallet with all my credit cards, my ID, and my passport." He confessed.

"Oh, no." Her eyes widened. "That must be so inconvenient for you."

Inconvenient was not a strong enough word to describe it.

One of the women stood and Miss Romano stopped her with a raised hand. The woman sat back down.

4

"Are these clients waiting to talk to you?" Knox looked at the women and they smiled at him.

"They're not clients." She glanced at them sternly and the women quieted down. "Have you been to the police yet? What did they say?"

Knox dragged his attention back from the exchange between the travel agent and the women. "Yes and no." He rubbed the side of his neck. "I went to the police station, but that didn't work out too well. I was hoping you could come with me and help me file the report with the officer on duty."

She stared at him.

"Just to facilitate the translation."

"Oh, yes. They don't always have someone there who can speak English."

He'd found that out the hard way. It seemed that every other Portuguese spoke English until he'd needed one. Then, of course, he couldn't find anyone who knew enough of the language to help translate his report.

The older women rose from their seats and approached Knox and Miss Romano. Knox stepped back.

Miss Romano sighed. "Excuse me, please."

In hushed tones, she conversed with the women who gestured in his direction several times. Miss Romano shook her head more than once, but in the end she relented to whatever they'd asked and spoke to them for a few moments longer. Whoever they were, they acted like they knew the travel agent personally and not just through business.

Were they trying to talk her out of helping him? What was he going to do if she changed her mind about coming with him to the police?

Of all the days to have Mãe and Tia Mariana show up to go home with her, this was not a good one. They came by a few times a week so they could walk home together with Jacinta. Depending on the day, she either appreciated it or wished they'd give her some room. Today would have been better if they'd skipped the visit.

"He's such a nice looking young man, Jacinta," Mom said again.

"And his eyes are so beautiful." Tia Mariana was partial to blue-eyed young men.

"He's a client and you two have to be quiet, or I'll ask you to wait outside until I'm done helping him." Jacinta talked under breath while trying to keep her smile.

She sent them a look loaded with warning, hoping it would work for a few more minutes, then turned back to the client. Mr. Campbell was a surprise. She hadn't expected him to be this young. From his emails, she'd assumed he was an older man who'd need some guidance in a foreign city.

But he was young and good looking and had the bluest eyes she'd ever seen, and it was quite embarrassing that her mom and aunt wouldn't stop staring at him.

"So you just need me to come and interpret for you, Mr. Campbell?"

He shifted his attention from her mom and aunt who still stared at him very impolitely. "Please, call me Knox. And yes, that's all I need." Hesitation filled his eyes for a brief moment. "I realize this is out of the realm of your regular work as a travel agent, and I'll happily pay for your time. I'm hoping it won't take too long."

It most likely would take some time, considering the slow, laborious Portuguese bureaucracy. But she didn't want to dash his hopes and tell him otherwise unless she had to.

"I can certainly help you with that." As inconvenient as it would be to accompany him, she couldn't leave him to go to the police by himself when he'd come to ask her.

"Thank you so much," he said. When his expression bloomed in open relief, that was all the confirmation she needed to know she should help him.

She went around her desk. After saving several documents, she turned off the computer.

Mãe stood and approached her, with Tia Mariana on her heels. "What did you say that made him so happy?"

Jacinta flipped off the back lights. "He needs to file a police report and I'm going with him to help translate."

"Jacinta, that is so nice of you," Tia Mariana said with a huge smile in Mr. Campbell's direction.

Mãe nodded, her expression matching that of her sister-in-law.

Jacinta suppressed a sigh. These two were more than she could take at times. "Come on, I need to lock up," she said to them.

She addressed Mr. Campbell in English. "Mr. Campbell, let me introduce you to my mother, Celestina, and my aunt, Mariana. They're on their way home and just stopped by to say hello."

He shook their hands and smiled. "Olá."

Mãe and Tia Mariana started talking with him and he chuckled. "I'm afraid that's all I know."

Mr. Campbell excused himself, then stepped out and waited for her on the sidewalk.

"Are you going with him right now then?" Mãe asked her.

"Yes, I'm going now so he can get it done and move on. I'm sure he's anxious to get his wallet back, if at all possible."

Jacinta turned on the alarm and gently prodded her relatives out the door so she could lock up.

Tia Mariana stared at Mr. Campbell. "How soon will he go back to America?"

"I have no idea, Tia." Jacinta turned the key in the lock and slipped it into her purse. She pulled out her phone and googled the directions. "Mr. Campbell, the closest police station is about thirty minutes away on foot. Do you mind if we walk there?"

"I don't mind at all," he said lightly.

Tia Mariana turned to Mr. Campbell. "Why don't you come for dinner when you're done?" she said slowly and loudly.

His forehead wrinkled and he shrugged at Tia Mariana. "What did she say?"

"She invited you for dinner when you're done at the police station." Jacinta explained. She should have known Mãe and Tia Mariana wouldn't let Mr. Campbell leave without an invitation.

"What does the normal protocol say in a situation like this?" Mr. Campbell asked her.

"What protocol?"

"I read in a travel book about Portugal that it's impolite to turn down invitations. Is that true?"

Jacinta hid a chuckle behind her hand. "That's entirely up to you, Mr. Campbell. They'll survive if you turn them down."

He hesitated for a moment. "Would you tell her I'll have to wait and see how long it takes?"

Jacinta related back to Tia Mariana and Mãe, saying she'd keep them updated but making no promises. She couldn't gauge Mr. Campbell's reaction. Was he trying to politely get out of the invitation or did he want to go but was unsure of what Jacinta thought?

She said goodbye to her mom and aunt, then walked away in the opposite direction with Mr. Campbell beside her.

Did she want to bring him by for dinner? Tomorrow was a holiday and a lot of the extended family would be at the house tonight.

How would he react to the crazy chaos of the Romano family?

CHAPTER TWO

$\mathcal{J}$acinta was right. Filing the police report took longer than it should. Being a Thursday night on the eve of a major national holiday didn't help either. Questionable characters of all ages passed through the lobby of the police station, some of them lingering nearer and longer than she wished. Several times, Mr. Campbell pulled his chair closer to her in a protective fashion. She couldn't make up her mind if the gesture was gallant or condescending.

The waiting was awkward. Somehow, word got out through the family network that she was at the police station with an American man, and two of her cousins, José and Nuno, stopped by nonchalantly. The family reach was legendary. She shouldn't be surprised at all to see her cousins checking on her to report back to her parents. She shook her head before they approached closer but Knox Campbell had caught the exchange. He held back any questions, but he must have many.

Mom texted her every few minutes to check on their progress, insisting she bring Mr. Campbell home for the family dinner. Jacinta disregarded the messages, but when they exited the police station a couple of hours later, cousin Paulo was waiting for them across the street in the taxi that he drove part-time.

Mr. Campbell took her hand and shook it. "I can't thank you enough for your help." He winced. "I'm sorry it took so long. Are you sure I can't pay you for your time?"

She waved off his apology. "Don't worry about it. It was out of your control. And no payment is necessary."

Her phone rang. It was the ring tone she'd assigned to Mãe. Cousin Paulo honked the horn from the and looked at the m other side of the street. She ignored them both an in front of her. Did he have any plans or even a place to stay? She'd added the agency's address and phone number to his contact information on the report, but he hadn't shared the purpose of his visit to Porto.

The horn honked again.

Mr. Campbell turned to look then shifted his backpack. He was hesitant to go; that much was obvious.

"Would you like to come for a late dinner, Mr. Campbell? If you don't have any plans already," she added.

He raised an eyebrow. "With you?"

Jacinta's cheeks heated. "With me, yes. And the rest of my big, loud family."

Across the street, the horn blared one more time.

"We usually get together at my grandparents' house on the last Friday of every month, but since tomorrow is a holiday, we're meeting today. You're welcome to join us—unless you mind hoards of intrusive, overprotective relatives. In which case, I recommend you turn me down."

He smiled wide, the dimples on his cheeks deepening into brackets. "Not at all. It sounds entertaining."

Blue eyes and dimples. An irresistible combination.

"Come on, my cousin is waiting for us." Jacinta gestured to the taxi.

His forehead wrinkled for a moment but when she crossed the street, he followed her.

Just as she climbed in the back seat, her other cousins who'd been around the police station scrambled in with her, effectively sandwiching her in the middle.

Mr. Campbell's eyes widened and he opened this mouth to say something, but she spoke first. "These are my cousins, José and Nuno. They're getting a ride back with us."

"I'm pretty sure I saw those two at the police station," Mr. Campbell said as he got in the front seat.

She nodded. "Yes, they were there." That was her family—inopportune and nosy. She jabbed the cousins with her elbows and they scooted away, complaining.

José and Nuno were a few years older than Jacinta and didn't speak much English. The ride to the family home was quiet, bordering on awkward.

When they arrived, the street parking was full as usual, and Paulo let them out at the corner while he went around to park in the back alley. The front of the building had all the windows on the ground floor lit, and the upper windows swung open to let in the evening breeze.

The others went in. Jacinta hung back and Mr. Campbell stayed with her on the sidewalk.

She gathered her courage. "Before we go in, I need to warn you that my family is crazy."

The corners of his lips rose, his bright eyes flashing at her. "I think all families have some kind of crazy."

They all said that. Jacinta shook her head. "Not like my family."

When she was at the university, she'd gone out with a few guys. Of course, the family had insisted she bring them over, and sometimes she had, curious to see what would come of it. She'd warned the very few who'd braved family dinners over the past few years, and most of them, if not all, hadn't taken her warnings seriously. Invariably, none of them had been able to deal with her peculiar family. Natural selection, Avó Teresa would say. Funny how grandmothers were always right.

But Mr. Campbell was a client, not a date. This was not the same kind of situation, yet it was hard to hold back from comparing.

When they came through the entrance, the front room was full as usual on such a family night event. Jacinta kept walking, waving at some of the cousins but not stopping to give explanations. Everyone probably already knew about the American guy she'd brought home with her, and those who didn't would know soon enough.

She glanced over her shoulder to make sure he followed her to the kitchen. Mãe stood at the side counter, sliding leftover sauce into a glass container, and Tia Mariana scrubbed a large pot at the sink. They both quickly finished their tasks when they saw her. Cousin Manuela swept the floor at the opposite corner.

"Jacinta, you're back!" Mãe wiped her hands on the edge of her apron.

Tia Mariana put the pot in the bottom cupboard. They turned their gazes from her to Mr. Campbell who'd stopped at the door, as if trying to decide whether to come in or stay where he was. He glanced between them, and they smiled back unabashedly.

Jacinta refrained from laughing. All it took was a blue-eyed guy with dimples to make a couple of senior-aged women embarrass themselves.

His neck flamed at the attention.

"You two are impossible. Look at the poor guy."

His ears had reddened into a deep hue.

Mãe grabbed two plates from the cupboard. "Ask him if he likes spaghetti and meatballs."

Jacinta hung her sweater and purse in the small service closet. "You can hang your backpack in here,

Mr. Campbell. It'll be safe. The restroom is down the hallway to the right, and we'll be eating outside on the back patio. Do you like spaghetti and meatballs?" When she turned, he stood directly behind her.

His blue eyes seemed brighter up close, and she swallowed. She moved to pass by him, and he moved in the same direction, which brought them closer than before. They stared at each other for a moment.

"What are you two doing? Kissing in the closet?" Tia Mariana peeked around the jamb.

Her cheeks flushed. "Tia." Jacinta scrambled away from the cramped closet as fast as she could. "He's right here and he can hear you." She hissed in a low voice.

"Well, he doesn't speak any Portuguese, does he?"

"I do," Jacinta said. He'd probably understood what Tia Mariana had said from her smug expression.

Mr. Campbell hung his backpack and gave a small, lazy smile. "I would love spaghetti and meatballs, Miss Romano."

"Please, call me Jacinta," she said over her shoulder on the way to the back patio.

"Jacinta," he repeated in a soft voice.

The way he said her name made her stop and turn to him.

He met her eyes, as if to say he now had her attention. "You really must call me Knox."

She smiled. "Okay, Knox. Meet me outside when you're ready."

On the patio, a few of the younger cousins sat against the fence playing games on their phones.

At the long table, Pai, Avô António, and Avó Teresa played a game of cards at the front. At the back table, a few of her older cousins sat with their spouses and kids. She waved to the cousins and greeted her closer relatives with a quick kiss on the cheek.

Avó Teresa put her cards down and patted the chair next to her. "What is this I hear about an American guy?"

"What's his name?" Pai kept his eyes on the cards in his hand. "Where does he come from?"

"Where did you meet him?" Avô António piped up.

Jacinta took the chair next to Grandma. "His name is Knox Campbell and he's a client from the agency.

Dad glanced at her. "What did you call him?"

"His name is Knox," she repeated. "He's American. I don't know any more than that."

"Noques? What kind of a name is that?" Her dad asked with confusion stamped on his face.

"Não, Pai. K-N-O-X. But the K is silent," she repeated patiently. It was a hard pronunciation for a Portuguese-speaking person.

Dad shook his head. "Kind of weird, if you ask me."

"It's not his fault his parents called him that." She arched an eyebrow. "I should know about being saddled with a name I didn't choose."

"What are you talking about?" Dad put down two cards while keeping an eye on Grandma and Grandpa. "Jacinta is a beautiful name. It's from the family too."

"It's not what I would have chosen. Just saying."

Knox came out to the patio holding a plate in his hands, and Mom followed close with a pitcher of lemonade and two glasses on a tray. Tia Mariana came behind carrying another plate.

Jacinta stood and took the plate from her aunt. Knox sat on the chair to the other side, next to Jacinta. He smiled and greeted everyone, introducing himself.

She gestured to her family. "This is my father, Carlos Romano. My grandfather, António Romano, and my grandmother, Teresa. You already met my mother and aunt. Her husband, uncle Francisco, is my dad's brother." Tio Francisco sat at the other end of the table with Tio Luís and Tia Glória, and Jacinta introduced them as well.

Grandma Teresa waggled her eyebrows. "He's a charmer, isn't he?"

Jacinta looked between her grandma and Knox. Was he a charmer? That hadn't been her first impression, but she didn't know him. He'd been humble enough to ask for help, and she didn't know of many men in her family who would. He'd also been patient at the police station, not losing his temper or demanding special treatment.

His warm eyes and disarming smile were enough to charm her grandma, and he already had two fans in Mom and her aunt.

What kind of man was Knox Campbell?

CHAPTER THREE

$\mathcal{K}$nox took a sip of his lemonade and leaned back in his chair. He'd been trying to rein in his smile all night, but he couldn't. Going to the travel agency to ask Jacinta Romano for help had been his best idea of late. Not all his problems were resolved yet, but he had a good feeling that his luck was turning back to what it had been before the theft. He'd worry about the rest later.

For a guy who'd been raised with a single mother and no siblings, the workings of large families mesmerized Knox. The Romano family was extensive, noisy, and completely devoted to one another. He could feel the way they cared, even when they tried to disguise it, like the teenagers at the very back of the yard who were playing together while ignoring the rest of their family.

The outside patio was typical Portuguese and almost pulled of a tourist brochure. A long wooden table, flanked by chairs and benches, took center stage in the long space. Mature grape vines hung over the patio, supported by cement posts and metal wires in a controlled canopy of flat green leaves and budding clusters of grapes. A string of large lightbulbs peeked intermittently from above, illuminating the dark area.

Jacinta had told him everybody's names and he'd forgotten them already. Portuguese was a difficult language, and being among conversations he couldn't understand was much more frustrating than he'd thought.

Jacinta refilled his glass. "Knox, my dad and grand-parents are asking me what happened to you."

Knox put down his fork and pushed his empty plate away. "Oh boy."

Jacinta translated to them and they chuckled. She'd heard the story already, and as embarrassing as it was, he knew the kind of reaction they'd have, just as the policemen and Jacinta had reacted at the station.

They'd laugh even harder once they heard the whole story. "I was on my last day and I wanted to get a souvenir for my mom. You know that outdoor market in the center of town close to the tower? So I'm looking at this lovely tile work, I reach for my wallet, and I'm holding the souvenir on my other hand"—he raised his hands with his palms out— "and out of nowhere this kid on a skateboard zooms by and grabs it right out of my fingers."

Jacinta nodded and translated again. Her grand-mother's eyes widened but the men were less delicate and laughed, shaking their heads.

Knox joined them in the nodding. "He wore jeans and a black hoodie pulled over his head and I couldn't even describe him." It had definitely not been a heroic tale. "So there I am, just watching the guy zip farther and farther away with my ID, my credit cards, and my passport, and there was noth-ing I could do."

Jacinta kept translating, entertaining them with his tale of woe.

Her grandmother spoke what sounded like a question.

Before Jacinta could translate for him, a guy came through the door and everyone greeted him warmly, the men slapping him on the back and the women kissing his cheeks. He was in his early thirties and a bit taller than most Portuguese men Knox had met. He had a word and a smile for everyone, and even the children ran to him, exchanging high-fives and fist bumps. Who was this guy?

Jacinta stood from her chair, and smiled. "Here's Matias."

When the man approached the table, he greeted the older people first then he brought an arm around Jacinta's shoulders and kissed the top of her head. Jacinta gave him a side hug and smiled at him warmly. She gestured at Knox, across the table, and said a few words in Portuguese.

I'm Matias." The guy extended his hand. "How are you?" He pulled a chair and sat between Jacinta and her grandmother.

He spoke English as well as Jacinta did, but who was he? Jacinta's boyfriend? Maybe her fiancé? They seemed close. Knox didn't see a ring on either one, but that didn't mean they couldn't be in a relationship. He could very well be her husband.

He held out his hand. "Knox Campbell. Your wife was kind enough to help me—"

Matias interrupted, an eyebrow raised. "My wife?"

Jacinta covered a smile behind her hand. Someone in the room said something and they all burst laughing. What was so funny? Sometimes not understanding the language was more than a little inconvenient.

Jacinta patted the guy's hand. "Matias is my cousin. We grew up together." She gestured at the group in the patio. "We're all family."

Knox's neck heated. Cousins. Not husband and wife. Embarrassment coursed through him, mingled with a clear sense of relief. He didn't want to think why he was so relieved to find out Jacinta was not married. He'd analyze that later.

"I'm sorry," he said with a sheepish smile.

Jacinta waved him off. "Oh, you're fine. Matias will make a fine husband one day, but not for me."

Her grandmother asked something and when Jacinta replied, they all laughed again.

Knox hunched a shoulder and smiled. "They're going to rib me about it, aren't they?"

Her cousin chuckled and Jacinta joined him. "Yes, it'll be a hard one to forget."

By now, Jacinta's mother and aunt, who'd gone back inside with their empty plates, returned to the rest of the family. Jacinta related his story to her cousin Matias. After watching them interact, Knox could see the family resemblance. He also noticed the lack of romantic feelings between them. They treated each other like siblings. She wasn't married to this guy, but that didn't mean she didn't have a boyfriend.

Knox forced his thoughts from the direction they wanted to go. Where was this interest in Jacinta's love life coming from? He'd barely met her and shouldn't be feeling this pull toward her.

"So, Knox, what is your plan?" Matias asked.

"I was able to file the police report." He nodded in Jacinta's direction and she gave him a thumbs-up. "My next step is to go to the embassy in Lisbon, so I can apply for a new passport. But I found out that tomorrow is a holiday and the embassy is closed, which means I have to wait till Monday." Another stumbling block to fixing his mess and returning home. "I had to cancel my credit cards, but I have some cash to tide me over while I wait for the new passport."

"How long will that take?" Jacinta asked.

"Two weeks." He'd called the embassy and pleaded with them, but emergency passports had a two-week turnaround, and nobody could change that.

Matias put his glass down on the table. "Do you have a place to stay?"

"No, not yet." Knox had been focused on filing the paperwork and talking to the embassy and hadn't spent much time thinking about the rest. Luckily, he still had his phone which had been securely inside his front pocket at the time of the theft.

Matias exchanged a look with Jacinta, lending evidence to the close bond they had between them. This was the kind of sibling relationship Knox had craved all his life. He'd always longed for a sibling or even a parent to be truly close to. He and his mom had a bond more out of necessity than conscious choice, their relationship fraught with tension. Her mental problems had dominated their lives and forced him to take on responsibility at a young age. They'd made it work, but it had never felt like family in any sort of the traditional sense. And it had always been lonely.

Though his mom was mostly stable now, living in a group home and holding a job, he didn't trust her and couldn't ask her to wire emergency money. He'd have to think of something else.

What would it be like to have someone in his life he could trust as much as Jacinta and her cousin Matias trusted each other?

A question passed from Matias to Jacinta without any words. She nodded back at him in reply.

"I'm leaving on a trip on Monday," Matias said.

"Matias is a river cruise captain and his trips take eight days," Jacinta added.

Knox hesitated for a moment, not sure why they shared this kind of information with him.

Jacinta glanced at her cousin one more time, and when she nudged him with her elbow, he chuckled lightly.

Knox's confusion must have been clear to see.

"You can stay at my apartment since I'll be away," Matias said.

CHAPTER FOUR

$\mathcal{K}$nox stood at the window, watching the street below, a cup of coffee in his hand.

Matias lived a couple of streets away from the building where Jacinta's parents lived, on the second story overlooking a square and a church. The day was just beginning to stretch in long rays of pale colored sun, and it promised to be a beautiful, warm one.

Knox had slept well, free of worries about what had happened and what the next few days would bring. He could only do so much while he waited, and worrying about what he couldn't control wouldn't change anything. Working for himself as a web developer had its advantages, and he was glad he could rearrange his schedule when emergencies arose.

Matias came in the kitchen and handed him a key. "Here. I'll be in and out until I leave on Sunday evening. Just make sure you lock the door when you leave. There isn't much food in the pantry or the

27

refrigerator"— he grimaced— "but you're welcome to go down to my grandma's and eat there. She's always feeding everyone."

Knox took the key and added it to his key chain. "Does she live close by?"

Matias pulled a small espresso from the automatic machine. He stirred it for a few moments and then downed it in one gulp. "Yeah, that's where we were yesterday."

"I thought Jacinta's parents lived there."

Matias set the small cup on the counter. "Her parents live on the second floor, grandparents on the first floor. Jacinta has the attic apartment." He gestured out the window in the opposite direction. "My parents, Luís and Glória, live ten minutes away. They'll be there today too. In fact, the whole family will be there to help with the preparations for the upcoming party."

Knox rinsed his cup in the sink. "Is that another holiday?"

"It will be for the Romanos." Matias smiled. "My grandparents are celebrating their sixtieth anniversary in a couple of weeks. Everyone's coming. It'll be huge. Anyway, you can go there for meals. There's always someone cooking." Matias drew out his phone. "Let me give you my number, just in case."

"I can't thank you and your family enough for being so generous," Knox said as he recorded Matias's number.

Matias left after explaining how to operate the washer. Knox did his laundry, waited for the machine to go through the cycle, then hung his clothes on the line. He'd gone for his suitcase which he'd left at the hotel, and was glad to have the chance to wash his clothes. It still amazed him how welcoming the Romano family was, especially Matias who'd brought him into his apartment without hesitation.

When Knox arrived at the other building, he knocked lightly. One of the teenagers opened the door and then screamed for Jacinta as she disappeared down the hallway. Jacinta finally showed up a few minutes later.

"Knox, don't just stand there. Please come in." She turned back and yelled in Portuguese toward the inside of the house. "Excuse my cousin Anita for not inviting you in. She has no manners."

Knox followed Jacinta just as he had the day before.

She continued. "I need your phone number." She glanced back at him over her shoulder. "So we can text you while you're at Matias's place. He doesn't have a land line. Does your phone work here?"

He nodded. "Yes, I got international service."

The kitchen was in a flurry of activity. Some of the younger women fed their children at a small table in the far corner, while other women stood at the stove and sink. Out on the patio, the older folks sat around the long table among cups of coffee, baskets of bread, and saucers of butter. Everyone waved at him and greeted him in Portuguese.

Jacinta gestured through the doors. "Go have breakfast. How do you like your coffee?"

"I had an espresso earlier with Matias."

She turned from the machine in the corner. "A latte then?"

A few minutes later, she joined him at the patio table and set down a large cup and saucer in front of him. "There you go." She drew two packets of sugar from her pocket and set them on the table.

"Obrigado," Knox said, enunciating the word slowly.

Everyone around them looked up and cheered. One of the kids gave him a high-five and Jacinta's father slapped him on the back. Her grandmother said something to Jacinta.

Jacinta smiled wide at him. "She said you'll be speaking like the rest of us by the time you go home."

He shook his head and held his hands up. "No, no, no. Portuguese is a very hard language."

Jacinta related it to her grandma who nodded at him.

When breakfast was done, Knox offered to help with the dishes and ended up beside Jacinta at the sink.

"Your family is so…"

"Obnoxious." She offered with a shrug. "I know. I'm sorry."

"No, not obnoxious at all." Knox turned to her. "Everyone has been so nice to me. And your cousin Matias gave me a key to his apartment this morning." Knox was impressed with the Portuguese hospitality. People were open and welcoming, and truly genuine.

Jacinta handed him another plate to wipe down. "Matias is great." She lowered her voice. "He's my favorite cousin. Don't tell anyone."

"You're not the same age, are you?"

"No, he's five years older than me, but we're the only ones among the cousins who don't have siblings. Our dads are brothers and they're very close. The story goes that Matias was really protective of me when I was born. We're more like brother and sister than cousins."

Her mother and grandmother came in and talked to Jacinta for a few minutes. She herded them out the kitchen, and after a bit of back and forth, they left with a wave. They smiled at him, and said something with a very strong accent.

"That word they said at the end, were they trying to say my name?" He set the last saucer on the drying rack.

Jacinta chuckled. "They're calling you Noques." She spelled it. "I'm sorry. They're having the hardest time with your name. It's difficult for them to say."

He could agree with that considering the Portuguese alphabet didn't even have the letter _K_.

Jacinta finished sweeping and hung the broom behind the door. "So today is a national holiday. It's called Day of Portugal. It's celebrated with parades, military demonstrations, and merit awards among other activities. We usually go see one of the parades downtown. Do you have any plans for today?"

"No plans at all." He didn't have to go anywhere until Monday.

She locked the door to the patio. "You don't have to hang out with us, you know."

"I want to hang out with you. And your family," he quickly added. As much as he liked Jacinta's family, he liked Jacinta more. The thought slammed into him and his ears burned. She could probably see right through him, but he wouldn't take back what he'd said. He did want to spend time with Jacinta, and her family was just as fun, despite her reluctance in admitting it.

He'd enjoy them while he could, both her company and her family's hospitality.

Jacinta climbed the stone bench and shaded her eyes to look over the sea of people lining up both sides of the street.

Knox stood beside her, scanning over the heads of most people around them.

"We always meet for the parade at this spot, but I can't see anyone." Jacinta hopped down.

She drew the cell out of her pocket. She swiped at the screen but there was no response. "I won't be able to call anyone. I forgot to charge my phone." She'd left her charging cord behind in her room when she went down to the kitchen and had forgotten to go back for it.

Knox handed her his phone. "Here, you can use mine."

"Wouldn't that be an international call for you?"

"I'm more worried about your family knowing where you are than international charges."

He made a valid point. They walked to the opposite side of the street where it was less crowded. She called Mãe and found out the family had moved on to a different meeting spot. Grandma and Tia Mariana tried to offer suggestions over the phone, and in the end, Jacinta and Knox decided to walk back home.

Knox was such an easy-going guy. Nothing seemed to upset him and he just adapted to whatever circumstance he was in. He'd also helped with the breakfast dishes and, other than Matias, none of the guy cousins ever wanted to be caught in the kitchen, as they relegated domestic chores to women's responsibility.

How was Knox not married? For sure he had to have a girlfriend.

"Were you able to call your family and tell them why your trip was delayed?" She asked him.

Walking in the opposite direction of everyone else going to the activities in the historic center, they descended the streets toward the river.

"I sent a message to my mom so she wouldn't worry, and I work for myself, which means no boss."

"That's it?"

"That's it what?" He slowed down and raised an eyebrow.

"Is there no one else you have to call?" Her cheeks heated and she looked ahead. Could she be any more obvious in her interest?

A lazy smile pulled at the corner of his mouth, and his glorious dimples made an appearance. "I have no other family but my mother, and no girlfriend to update."

She nodded, not knowing what to say to dispel the awkward moment and disguise her curiosity.

"And you?" he asked. "If you were to be stranded in a foreign country because you were so distracted a kid stole your wallet and passport, who would you call?"

"That's an oddly specific scenario." She tapped her chin. "I'd call my family, of course." Was he trying to find out if she had a boyfriend?

"Yes, after you talked to your parents, and grand-parents, and your cousin Matias, and everyone else." He made a wide arc with his arms and then slipped his hand in his pockets, the same lazy smile on his lips. "Anyone special you'd have to call? A boyfriend? A fiancé?"

Jacinta shook her head slowly. "No one special like that. No boyfriend and definitely no fiancé." Most guys didn't appreciate meddling families who insisted on keeping up with her dating life.

Knox's expression softened into a wide smile, and he nodded slowly, apparently satisfied with her reply.

When Jacinta looked up, she was surprised to notice they had ended up in front of the Dom Luís bridge. "Would you like to walk to the other side?"

CHAPTER FIVE

*K*nox looked up as people strolled around them in both directions. "I didn't realize it was open for pedestrians." The arched metal bridge seemed familiar. "Is this the one designed by Eiffel?"

Jacinta smiled. "You've been reading those brochures I emailed you, haven't you?"

"I didn't have time to visit all of the places, but I did look over all the materials you sent."

He'd felt compelled to read all the emails she'd sent his way, since he had asked for suggestions in the first place.

"It's shared with the above-ground metro." She went on. "The tracks lead in and out of the station. The conductors drive slowly and honk to warn the pedestrians."

The sidewalk was wide enough for them to walk side by side and Knox kept to Jacinta's left. When they reached the center of the bridge, they stopped and viewed the river and the cities on both sides. To the north, the city of Porto inched up the hills in a mass of red-roofed buildings and white-faced monuments; to the south, the modern city of Vila Nova de Gaia shared the same colored roofs but less historic buildings.

On the river, boats of different sizes lined the banks on both sides, like parenthesis holding back the secret to an adventure.

"Do you see that ship down there?" Jacinta stepped closer to Knox and rested a hand on his forearm.

He stilled at her touch. She stood close enough that he could smell her floral scent—something fresh and full of simple goodness. The warmth of her skin tripped his heartbeat, and for a moment, nothing else was as important as sharing the same space with her.

"Do you see it?" she said again.

With difficulty, Knox dragged his attention to her extended hand and tried to concentrate on what she said. "Which one?"

"The longest one, all white and flat-topped."

"With the rows of cabin windows?"

"The very one. That's Matias's ship. It's the newest and most luxurious in the fleet, and it even has a swimming pool on top." Jacinta sighed.

"Have you been aboard?"

"Not for a trip, but Matias gave me a tour. It's absolutely amazing." Jacinta stepped away from him and crossed her arms over the railing.

Knox wasn't ready for the loss of contact between them. What would she do if he took her hand and they walked together like a couple? Everywhere around them, couples of all ages held each other's hands, their smiling faces and intimate expressions drawing out a side of Knox he hadn't felt before—part longing and part envy for something he didn't have.

A maudlin thought, undoubtedly brought on by the beautiful river-front scenery and the eagerly curious woman with a kind heart.

Knox retrieved his phone from his pocket and took a picture of the view.

As they resumed walking, a group of Korean tourists marched between Knox and Jacinta, splitting them apart. She shrugged back at him, and changed directions, stepping toward the barrier between the sidewalk and the Metro tracks. He tried to catch up, but more and more tourists carried her farther from his side.

From behind, the rumbling of a Metro train approaching caught his attention. Knox kept an eye on Jacinta's head, trying not to lose her amid the many other dark-haired pedestrians.

As the crowd got thicker, a group of teenagers bumped her toward the track. Anxiety filled his chest. Knox called to Jacinta, and she looked back over her shoulder. He sprinted, dodging the bodies in his way.

When the train honked, Jacinta startled. Other people jumped away from the tracks and jostled her back in his direction but not quite far enough. Knox reached out his arm forward and yanked the back of her shirt. With the momentum, she slammed into his chest just as the train zoomed by the exact spot where she'd been. His arms came around her back and he held her close, both of them trembling at the possibility of what had almost happened. Jacinta rested her face against him, her rapid, shallow breaths fanning across his shirt and warming his gooseflesh skin.

Knox didn't move for a few moments. He needed to cherish Jacinta in the safety he could now provide, not knowing if he did it for her comfort or his peace of mind, or maybe even both. It had been a close call: a few extra seconds or too many inches out of reach, and the reality would have been much different.

A young couple tapped Jacinta's shoulder. She turned to face them without leaving his embrace. The guy said something with a solemn expression, then they nodded and strolled on, their arms around each other.

"What did he say?"

Jacinta looked up at him. "He said you saved me just in time."

Jacinta stayed in Knox's embrace as her heartbeat slowed from the crazy gallop it had taken. He rested an arm around her shoulder, pulling her to his side as they resumed walking. When the flat cement sidewalk transitioned to irregular cobblestones, Knox slid his arm down and took her hand, interlacing their fingers. His grip was tight, and she held on to him with the same fierceness, finding comfort in the connection.

They walked in silence to the end of the bridge and continued on into a garden of olive trees and park benches full of people. On the other side of the garden, under the branches of a gnarled tree, they found an empty bench. Knox veered in its direction and when they sat together, his arm came around her once more.

Knox had saved her life.

When the group of Korean tourists walked by, the crowd had been so thick that Jacinta had been jostled away from the sidewalk. The Metro had come too fast.

If not for Knox's quick reaction, she would have been gravely injured, if not worse.

Knox took a deep breath, his chest expanding. Somehow, it didn't feel awkward to be sitting this close to a man she'd met only yesterday, holding her gently in the twilight hour as if they'd been familiar long before today. When at last her heartbeat returned to its normal rhythm, Jacinta straightened, breaking the closeness. His hand rested lightly around her back with a hand on her shoulder, as if he were reluctant to completely let go.

She broke the silence first. "This is the first time I don't mind sitting on this side of the garden. The view from here is so ugly." Only rooftops and old buildings, unlike the riverview side.

"Not to me."

Jacinta looked up to find Knox watching her. The reality of what had almost happened slammed into her and tears gathered in the corners of her eyes. "If you hadn't been there…"

"But I was and I—"

He turned his head away and closed his eyes, then swallowed hard.

Whatever he'd been about to say, he'd changed his mind.

It was for the best. The intensity of the moment had created a false sense of intimacy between them. Nothing more.

They found their way to the riverfront and had dinner at an outdoor restaurant. Knox told her about growing up in a small New Jersey community and walking through a neighborhood of Portuguese immigrants on his way to school. He talked fondly of the local bakery and of the friends he'd meet there on the walk back home.

Jacinta told him of growing up with a gaggle of crazy boy cousins who constantly pulled pranks on her. Matias had been her defender, helping to forge their close bond at an early age.

They talked of books and movies, of their jobs and their hobbies. They talked away the minutes into hours until time stood still, and the moments stretched into forever. How could she capture such fleeting happiness and brand the magic into her heart? How could she even try?

The man in front of her was not the same one she'd met yesterday. He'd become much, much more.

A waxing moon perched shyly in the dark sky when Jacinta and Knox arrived at her street. The taxi they'd called pulled up to the curb, and Knox held the door open for her. They'd lost track of time, absorbed in each other as they'd been all night, and the church clock two streets over clanged the second hour.

Jacinta turned the key noiselessly and they slipped into the darkened foyer, leaving a crack in the front door.

Knox took a step and rested a hand on her arm. "I never had a day—and a night—like this before." He spoke softly.

She could barely discern his eyes but the warmth of his body, and his fingers on her arm, raised a swarm of feelings inside her that wouldn't settle. Jacinta moved into his space and his arms brought her closer still. His other hand caressed the contour of her cheek, trailing a line of fire to her lips.

She felt him close the distance and she tipped her face to him.

"Jacinta, is that you?" A light flicked on in the next room and Avó Teresa's shuffling steps followed behind.

Knox stepped away from Jacinta with a heavy sigh, and she understood his frustration. "Yes, I'm locking up, Avó. I'll be right there."

Jacinta tugged at the door handle and Knox slipped by her, resting his hand on top of hers before stepping from the stoop to the sidewalk.

"Can I see you tomorrow?" he asked, with a smile in his voice.

The incandescent light from the single bulb over the door turned his eyes a warm, dark blue.

"You mean today?" Jacinta leaned forward. "Come for breakfast when you're ready."

Knox brushed a kiss on her cheek. "I wouldn't miss it for anything."

Neither would she.

CHAPTER SIX

*K*nox woke early on Monday morning. The sun wasn't up yet. He'd left the blinds open and a pale pink hue bathed the wall next to the bed.

Matias had left the night before for his week-long cruise. Just as he was closing the door, he'd come back and asked Knox what his intentions were toward Jacinta.

Knox had thought for a moment. He couldn't deny he had feelings for Jacinta. As much as he'd tried to disguise it, no doubt his expression gave him away. It was impossible not to smile whenever he was around her. And it wasn't his fault his eyes followed her constantly, even when they were in a crowd. He'd found her pretty when he had met her, but he'd become much more attracted to her with each passing day, to her warm chocolate eyes and her gentle features.

He'd come for breakfast on Saturday morning and had spent all weekend with the Romano family, side by side with Jacinta, helping her with the preparations for her grandparents' sixtieth anniversary. The party was two weeks away, and they were expecting extended family to come from all corners of the country. The women in the family started preparations a whole month before, and this weekend had only been part of all the cooking and baking and freezing they needed for the final day. In the evening, he and Jacinta sat at the back of the patio, and talked for hours.

He'd only known her for a few days, and the more time he spent with her, the more he looked forward to it. Unfortunately, they hadn't had a private moment to share a kiss, and Knox was dying to kiss Jacinta.

Matias must have seen the interest on his face and had read between the lines of what Knox had kept to himself. He'd told Knox to look out for Jacinta, reminding him she had a large, protective family. As if Knox could forget that detail.

Jacinta had asked him not to mention the near-accident on the bridge to anyone. Not that it was a secret, but maybe she wanted to keep the moment between the two of them, just as he did. The experience had been too intense, and sharing it with someone else would take away the magic of the moment that followed and the strength of the memories. It was more special between them alone.

Today Knox was going to Lisbon to apply for a passport. He was leaving on the early train and returning as soon as he was done. Jacinta had tried convincing him to stay overnight at another cousin's apartment—she had cousins all over the country—and come back the next day after some sightseeing. He'd told her he didn't want to inconvenience another cousin of hers, unwilling to confess she was the reason he wanted to return as soon as possible. A whole day without seeing her would be long enough already.

Upon returning, he'd have to wait for two weeks until the new passport came so he could finally go home. He scrubbed his face and drew the curtains aside.

What was he going to do for two whole weeks to occupy his time?

His chest constricted. Two weeks with Jacinta were not enough.

CHAPTER SEVEN

$\mathcal{T}$he party for Avó Teresa and Avô António's anniversary had been going all afternoon and evening. Jacinta looked across the patio where Knox sat on a bench with some of the teenage cousins. As if sensing her, he raised his eyes and smiled. She smiled back.

The little stolen moments between Knox and her had been too few and far between in the past two weeks. Everything else had taken too much of her time, and her family had monopolized more of her attention than she'd wanted to give them. Not that she didn't want to help, but she'd found herself falling for Knox a little more each time they went for walks, and those had been insufficient. As soon as he got his passport, he'd return home, and Jacinta wasn't ready to say goodbye.

As if lending a hand in the kitchen cleaning hadn't been plenty, Knox had offered his business skills as well. He'd updated the agency's website, and had developed new software for Tia Glória's hair salon. Her younger cousins had loved teaching Knox how to play real football, and he'd gone along with it, pretending their tips made a difference in his kicking skills. Even Dad and Avô António had taken to asking him over to play cards with them, a universal language that didn't need interpretation.

How had Knox come to fit so well in her crazy family?

The backyard and patio were full to capacity. More tables and chairs had been brought in, and there was music and plenty of food laid out. In the kitchen, a replica of the wedding cake waited to be brought out, and her grandparents' anniversary would be celebrated by their descendants: seven sons and nineteen grandchildren, not to mention spouses, cousins, and friends. Not everyone had been able to come, but most had, and Jacinta knew how much that meant to her grandparents.

Grandma scooted her chair closer to Jacinta's. "That boy of yours, Jacinta. He can't keep his eyes off of you."

Jacinta turned her gaze from him and looked to Avó Teresa. "He's twenty-six, avó. That makes him a man. But he's not my man." A small pang of something she didn't want to identify squeezed in her chest.

"You know his age." Avó said with a small smile and a knowing look.

Jacinta also knew his birthday, which kind of cereal he liked for breakfast, and how he spent his Saturday mornings volunteering. They'd talked about a lot of things, but but she still had so much to learn about Knox. They could talk every day for the rest of the year, and she'd still be craving more.

"Did he kiss you yet?"

She turned to Grandma and arched an eyebrow. "As if he's had the chance." She should have known this kind of questioning was coming. Avó Teresa was too direct to worry about privacy.

Grandma winked at her. "You've surely spent time together."

But not enough time alone to create the right mood for kissing. Not since the night of the holiday when Avó Teresa had unintentionally interrupted them. Jacinta scoffed. "The way Dad looks at him, I wonder Knox still has the courage to talk to me."

"He makes up for it by looking at you every few minutes." Grandma Teresa chuckled lightly.

"It won't matter. Knox is leaving on Wednesday, remember?" Two and a half weeks had gone by too fast.

"Already? That's come faster than I thought."

When Jacinta chanced a glance in his direction, she found him looking at her. Her cheeks warmed and her heart skipped a beat.

Grandma Teresa patted her arm. "It'll be okay, Jacinta. If it's meant to be, it'll work out."

Was it meant to be? How could they work it out with an ocean between them?

Grandma Teresa stood and walked over to Tia Glória, leaving Jacinta to her thoughts of impossible dreams and love without a chance. She blinked, forcing away the tears that lingered too close. She wouldn't cry about it. Not yet.

"What's going on in your mind, Jacinta?" Matias pulled up the chair on the other side and sat down. "You look miserable."

She pushed her melancholy away and smiled at Matias. "Nothing in particular."

"You could probably fool someone else, but not me." He glanced to Knox and then back at her. "When is he leaving?"

She pulled up her legs and wrapped her arms around them. "He changed his ticket to early Wednesday morning."

"So he got his new passport?"

"It's arriving tomorrow by special courier." Her voice caught and she cleared her throat.

"You still have two whole days left."

Jacinta nodded.

"Have you two had a chance to talk about things?"

"Not yet." If she had the courage to bring anything up, she might ask Knox to sit down and talk. But that sounded too much like a define-the-relationship conversation, and what right did she have to bring that up?

At the other end of the patio, her cousins, Carlos, Nuno, and Paulo slapped Knox on the back. Knox straightened, as if gathering his courage, and exchanged high-fives with the three youth, before heading her way. As soon as he turned his back, the cousins started laughing. What was going on?

"Those three are up to something." Jacinta rose from her chair and headed in his direction.

"I'm right behind you," Matias said.

Knox stopped in front of grandma Teresa and cleared his throat. "Gosto de cheirar os meus peidos," he said loudly.

Avó Teresa froze.

Jacinta's eyes widened and she covered her mouth.

For a moment, all conversation stopped on the patio, and the heavy quiet stood in contrast to the music still coming from the speakers. Then everyone burst into laughter.

Knox turned red. Then he bowed to Avó and stepped back just as Jacinta reached him. Everyone clapped and laughed some more.

She looped her arm through his. "Let's go for a walk, Knox."

He covered her hand with his. "Great idea."

Out of the corner of her eye, she saw Matias take the troublemakers aside, hopefully to get the scolding they deserved.

Jacinta unlocked the back gate and they stepped into the side street behind the building. Other than a few people to the other end, it was deserted. She guided Knox the opposite way.

"I didn't say 'Congratulations on sixty years of marriage', did I?"

"No, you didn't." Far from it.

He nodded. "I had a feeling I didn't, when everyone started laughing so hard. What did I say?"

Jacinta looked away to hide her smile.

Knox stopped and turned to her. "Come on, tell me."

The more she tried not to laugh, the more she did. "I'm sorry, Knox," she said between breaths. "Please know I'm not making fun of you."

He rubbed her arms, his expression bordering on amused. "I'm guessing it wasn't a swear word."

She shook her head. "I like to smell my farts." She started laughing again.

Knox's forehead wrinkled. "Excuse me?"

"That's what you said to my grandma. 'I like to smell my farts.'"

He closed his eyes. "I should have known."

Jacinta wiped her eyes and took a deep breath. "Why didn't you check Google Translate?"

He took her hand and resumed walking. "I did. But I asked them to read the sentence so I could get the pronunciation right, and they said it was all wrong."

"They're sixteen-year-old-boys. What did you expect?"

He smiled. "That's what I get for wanting to show off to you that I can learn Portuguese. I walked right into their trap."

Jacinta squeezed his hand and stopped in the middle of the street, facing him. "You want to learn Portuguese?"

Knox looked each way and then held on to both her hands. "Jacinta, I want everything to do with you. If it takes me three years to learn Portuguese, so be it. But I want to be able to talk to your family when I come back for a visit."

A tear escaped from the corner of her eye. "A visit?" she said softly.

He closed the distance between them. "Is it okay if I come back to see you?" He matched her tone.

Jacinta brought a hand up to his face and traced the dimple line on the side of his cheek. He caught her hand in his, closing his eyes. When his arms came around her, she stretched on tiptoes and met him halfway.

This was the kiss she'd been wanting since their first night out. And from Knox's reaction, he'd been wanting it as much. There was no hesitation between them, no first-time awkwardness, no trace of discomfort or uneasiness; only a deep sense of happiness and rightness.

A wave of bliss enveloped her heart as her lips molded to his mouth, and her arms wound around his neck.

Without even trying, she'd found the kind of love to hold on to forever.

CHAPTER EIGHT

Knox finished zipping his suitcase and wheeled it to the foyer.

Matias came out of the kitchen to meet him. "You're off then?"

"Yes, the plane leaves at eight-thirty. I need to get there two hours earlier."

He reached for his key chain, took off the key Matias had given him two and a half weeks before, and handed it back.

Knox offered his hand. "Thank you for everything. You took me into your apartment, and you didn't even know me."

Matias shook Knox's hand firmly. "I'm a good judge of character, and so are my relatives."

"I'm still in awe at how kind and welcoming your family is."

"Just don't trust a certain few teenagers who like to prank unsuspecting guests."

Knox chuckled. "I learned my lesson."

"I never thanked you for updating the agency's website," Matias said. "It looks great. Jacinta won't stop talking about it. And the software you developed for my mom's hair salon is just what she needed. I took a look at it. It's so simple and yet so effective."

"I'm glad it works for them." Knox had needed something to do, and working with Jacinta on both projects had been enough thanks. "It was the least I could do after everything your family has done for me."

When he reached the sidewalk in front of the building, Jacinta waited at the curb, the idling of her car the only sound in the early morning.

He placed the suitcase in the trunk and climbed in the passenger seat.

Jacinta held on to the wheel, a tremulous smile on her lips. Her eyes shone suspiciously bright and Knox's heart skipped a beat. His feelings mirrored the ones he saw in her face, the anxious tightness in his chest as the upcoming separation loomed closer.

Before fastening the seat belt, Knox leaned across the console and brought his arms around her, kissing her on the lips. She kept a hand on the wheel and returned the hug with the other arm.

"Jacinta, this is not goodbye." Another kiss. "How do you say in Portuguese when you'll see someone really soon?"

She wiped at the corner of her eye. "Até logo." Her expression softened.

With his fingers, Knox tilted her chin up. "This is até logo. Only até logo and not ever a goodbye."

She nodded quickly as another tear fell. "Only até logo," she repeated.

"We'll video chat as often as we can, okay?"

Another nod, and another kiss, this one a little longer and deeper. He was going to miss her so much.

Jacinta put the car into gear and drove away. He kept a hand on her shoulder. He'd have held her hand but she needed it to maneuver the clutch.

When they arrived at the upper departure deck at the airport, Jacinta pulled up to the curb. They'd already decided she would drop him off instead of parking and going in with him. He'd almost let her talk him into a few more minutes together, but it would have been harder for him, and he'd reminded her she did have to work that morning. In the end, she relented.

Knox retrieved his suitcase from the trunk and shouldered his computer bag. She came around and met him on the sidewalk. Immediately, their arms came around each other in a tight embrace. Knox bent over and kissed her long and tenderly, transferring all his feelings into the last kiss for a while.

"I love you," he said into her ear.

"I love you too."

Knox pulled back to look into her eyes and memorize the beautiful brown he'd come to love.

After another kiss he said, "Don't give up on me."

"I won't."

Before he lost his courage, Knox grabbed his suit-case and walked away.

CHAPTER NINE

*J*acinta tapped halfheartedly at the keyboard. She'd closed the agency for the lunch hour a few minutes before but hadn't felt like going home like she sometimes did. Lately, she preferred the solitude and kept herself apart from family gatherings as much as she could.

A knock sounded against the glass door. She should have pulled the blinds down instead of just turning the lights off. Whoever it was could probably see her sitting at her desk.

When the knock sounded again, she rose from her chair. It was Matias.

She unlocked the door and let him in, locking it again. "Hey, Matias." She leaned up for the customary kiss on the cheek. "What brings you here?"

"You bring me here, Jacinta. Why else would I have come?"

59

She shrugged and sat back down.

"Turn off the computer. We're going out to lunch."

Jacinta glared at him. "I don't want to go out to lunch. It's too hot outside."

"You've finally noticed the weather?"

Maybe she'd only kept to the apartment and the agency, and nowhere else, but she was aware of the weather and the passing of seasons. "You're so not funny, Matias."

He came around the desk and took over the mouse.

"Hey, I was working on that."

He let go and stepped back. "Save your work and turn it off. You're coming with me to lunch."

Jacinta grumbled but did as he asked.

Matias had his car close by and crossed the bridge to the Gaia side. He drove down to the river front and parked on the dock facing the *Princess Catarina*, the ship he captained.

A small, anemic thrill sparked in her chest. The ship had a four-star chef on the payroll, and it looked like Matias was taking her to eat there.

"You don't get sick of being aboard all the time?"

Matias arched an eyebrow at her and she immediately regretted the snark in her voice. He didn't deserve it.

No one else was aboard the ship, but a table was set at the far end of the lounge in the upper deck. The air conditioned room was a wonderful contrast from the hard August sun, and soft piano music played from the carefully disguised speakers in the ceiling.

Matias served them both a meal of grilled shrimp and dark greens salad with a white wine vinaigrette. For dessert, a chilled mango mousse was the decadent compliment to the lighter main course, and Jacinta took her time appreciating the sweet tartness and smooth texture.

"We should go to the movies this weekend before I leave on Sunday."

Jacinta licked her spoon until there was nothing left, biding her time to reply. "I'm not in the mood to be out in public."

"Do you want to go hiking on Saturday morning then? The exercise will be good."

"You're full of advice for me but it's been a long time since I've seen you date. How come? You're good looking, you've got a great head on your shoulders, and an interesting job." He should have girls lining up to meet him.

He shrugged. "I got tired of dating. And I had three girlfriends who didn't like my job."

"What you need is a girl who'll come with you on the ship."

He smirked. "Like that's going to happen."

"You just haven't met the right person yet."

"Maybe she isn't in Portugal," Matias said. "Maybe it will take an American to steal my heart."

"Don't mock me," Jacinta warned. "And Knox didn't steal anything." She'd given him her heart willingly. And look where that had left her—just as alone as Matias.

He turned to look out the sliding door at a seagull perched on the railing. "Sometimes I doubt I'll ever meet someone."

"Watch out, Matias. One of these days a girl will catch your eye, and you'll be head over heels for her before you know how it happened."

He chuckled. "We'll see, priminha."

Little cousin. That was the nickname he'd given her when she was born.

Matias took a sip of his espresso. "Okay, that's enough talk about me. Everyone's worried about this funk you're going through."

Jacinta's shoulders slumped. She knew her parents and grandparents had been trying to cheer her up, and while she'd put on a façade for a while, even that had been too much work to keep up with.

"I just need—" her voice trembled and she waited until the emotion passed. "I need a little time. That's all." It would take more than a little time, but she'd get over Knox Campbell one day. In time, he'd be a lovely memory she'd recall with both fondness and regret.

"I hate seeing you like this." Matias squeezed her shoulder. "When did you last hear from Knox?"

"Last week. He sent an email setting a time for video chat but he never came on." She'd waited all day.

"Maybe he's traveling for work and can't get in touch with you until he gets back."

She nodded at Matias. "I guess." She didn't want him to know that Knox had been on a trip a week after arriving home, and he'd still found a way to video chat with her. But in the past three weeks he'd started going every other day without talking to her, then a few days in between, and now it had been six days in a row.

He'd moved on, and she couldn't blame him. Long distance relationships were hard to keep. Absence didn't make the heart grow fonder, just lonelier.

She helped Matias clear the table and carry the dishes to the galley. As she filled the sink, she dropped utensils onto to the rubber mat on the floor.

Matias turned to her. "That was the third time."

"Was it? I'm sorry. I'm distracted."

"You know how it goes: you drop three things on the floor, it means someone wants to talk to you."

Matias had always had a propensity toward superstition and old wives' tales.

"Nobody wants to talk to me." She gave him a look that didn't invite discussion on the subject.

He drove her back to the agency, inching along downtown Porto's congested streets. Jacinta kept quiet and Matias seemed too focused on traffic to pay attention to anything else.

When they stopped at a red light, she caught Matias smirking. "What's going on?"

"I just saw a pregnant lady," he said.

Since when had he started noticing pregnant ladies? "And?" Jacinta prompted.

"Before that, I saw a man walking on crutches." He spared a quick glance her way, but didn't say anything.

Jacinta rolled her eyes and groaned. "Not that one."

Matias smiled. "A lame person—in this case a guy using crutches— followed by a pregnant person, is always followed by a person you know." He paused for effect which was completely wasted on her. "You'll see."

In a city this large, it was bound that, sooner or later, she'd be able to see someone in that order. Another silly expression.

"You're an oddball, Matias," she said to him with a teasing smile.

"But I'm still your favorite cousin." He winked at her.

He absolutely was. "Thank you for the wonderful lunch." Things didn't feel completely right, but Matias had brightened her day a little.

"Anytime, priminha." He kissed her cheek before leaving.

Jacinta spent the rest of the afternoon playing solitaire on the computer. She'd replied to all the client emails in the morning, and there were no upcoming reservations to take care of. At five minutes to seven, she turned off the computer, all the overhead lights, and unplugged the string lights around the window. One of these days, she'd take them down. They didn't look so festive anymore.

She stepped into the bathroom to wash her hands and wipe down the vanity.

"Boa tarde," a male voice said.

Her mouth tightened in a thin line, and her fists clenched. Heck, no. She would not be seeing a client this late in the afternoon. She was tired and hungry and wanted to go home and pick a good book to read. "We're closed," she said in a loud voice as she reentered the main room of the agency.

Her hands relaxed and her mouth dropped open. On the other side of her desk, Knox stood with a large smile on his face, his dimples in full bracket mode, and his adorable blue eyes twinkling at her.

"Knox?" She managed in a small voice, as the tears already queued in the corner of her eyes.

"Yes, it's me," he said to her in Portuguese.

"You can speak Portuguese too?"

He pinched his forefinger to his thumb and drew them apart a little. "Only this much but I'm getting better at it," he replied in English.

"You planned a visit and didn't tell me." As happy as she was to see him, Jacinta tried to push away her resentment at the lack of communication from him in the past week.

Knox stepped forward and took her hands. "It's more than a visit." He paused. "As soon as I got back last May, I started plans for a permanent transfer. It took me longer than I thought it would with all the paperwork and bureaucracy involved."

A permanent transfer? Jacinta blinked. "I haven't heard from you in six days. I thought you'd moved on."

His expression fell. "That long? I'm so sorry. I was so busy squaring everything away, putting my mom's affairs in order, and selling my furniture and car, I guess I lost track of time."

Jacinta held her breath. He'd sold everything. "You're not here for a visit."

Knox smiled, and the dimples she'd missed so much were back. "I'm here to stay, Jacinta. If you'll have me." He pulled his arms around her and bent to kiss her.

When his lips touched hers, Jacinta's world righted itself. She kissed him back and happiness soared inside her, flying higher and higher until she couldn't hold it in anymore. Her arms squeezed around him, and Knox held on to her tightly.

A pair of squeals sounded from the door. "Eu sabia! Eu sabia!" Mãe and Tia Mariana jumped excitedly in place like school girls.

Jacinta groaned and hid her face in Knox's chest. "Are you sure about this? You know I come with a crazy family."

He brushed her lips once more with the kind of kiss she'd never tire of. "I wouldn't have it any other way."

DEAR READER,

$\mathscr{T}$hank you so much for reading Knox and Jacinta's story, *Hold Me at Twilight*.. I hope you've enjoyed reading it as much as I enjoyed writing it. You may learn more about them and their story on Pinterest.

Please consider leaving a review on Amazon and Goodreads. This is the best way to support me as an author.

For news of upcoming books and promotions, join my readers club.

I love to hear from readers! You can email me at lucinda@lucindawhitney.com.

Thank you!

Want to find out how Matias and Vanessa met?

Turn the page to read *Meet Me at Sunrise*.

Read Matias and Vanessa's story
in *Meet Me at Sunrise*.

CHAPTER ONE

*T*his was a bad idea. Why had she let Grandfather talk her into this trip?

Vanessa stopped at the entrance of the ship's formal dining room and gazed around. Outside the panoramic windows, the city of Porto inched up the hill from the docks on the other side of the river, the buildings and roofs and church towers competing for space unsuccessfully. Myriad lights shone against the night sky and spilled in reflective ribbons on the water's surface. In its architectural disorganization, there was a beauty that called to her. It was a city so unlike the ones she was used to. Much of Portugal was still a mystery to her.

Inside, the passengers sat in groups of eight at round tables, and waiters in white coats flitted between them with silver platters and bottles of wine. Everything in the room spoke of elegance and luxury, from the furniture and dark wood trim to the

71

impeccably white tablecloths and fresh-cut flowers to the damask draperies drawn back with silver ropes and the pianist undulating at the baby grand.

She'd barely looked at the pamphlets Grandfather had sent her and was not prepared for the real-life opulence before her. She—the Kansas girl who preferred well-worn jeans and flip-flops to dresses and high heels—aboard the *MS Princess Catarina,* the crown jewel in Grandfather's fleet of luxury river ships. How long until someone recognized she didn't belong here?

A very bad idea indeed.

At least she was by herself. She'd managed to convince Grandfather she didn't need the bodyguard he'd planned to send with her. As president of a multi-million-dollar company, he was the one who needed bodyguards. She was just an American girl on her own, and nobody knew of her yet. Besides, what could possibly go wrong on a small cruise ship?

Inside her clutch, her phone rang. It was probably Dad. Again. He'd insisted on being able to contact her throughout the trip and had prearranged a new plan with Verizon. He'd have to wait until tomorrow to talk to her.

An appetizing scent reached her nose. Roasted pork, rosemary potatoes, and something else she couldn't identify. Vanessa was late to dinner and she had missed the "Welcome Aboard" cocktail party. The light breakfast from this morning was only a memory by now. Her stomach rumbled.

The maître d' appeared at her elbow. "May I have your name, please?"

Vanessa turned to him, grateful that English was the official language aboard. "Vanessa Clark. Is it open seating?" she asked, while he checked the list in front of him.

"Not for you, Miss Clark. Please follow me."

As he cut a path to the center of the dining room, Vanessa ignored the urge to smooth her dress and held on to her sequined clutch instead, carefully stepping on the gleaming wood floor and willing herself not to trip on her strappy sandals.

Was it her imagination or did most people pause to look at her? The conversations and clinking of silverware against the porcelain dishes continued on around them, as a few of the passengers darted their eyes at her. This was karma for being the last one to arrive at dinner. For someone who didn't like attention, she sure had a lot of it now.

The maître d' pulled out a chair next to a dark-haired man in a black uniform. He was clean-shaven and appeared to be in his early thirties, with an air of confidence that drew her attention. Who was he and what did he do?

The man stood and nodded at her. "Good evening, Miss Clark."

Her eyes widened for a moment. How did he know who she was?

He didn't smile openly, but his mouth curved into a pleasant expression, and Vanessa's lips rose in response.

"I'm glad you made it." His voice was deep and lightly accented, and his arresting brown eyes held hers for a moment longer than good manners called for.

After an awkward pause, they sat down and Vanessa dragged the bib-size napkin onto her lap, looking away from him and realizing the other guests at the table were staring at her. She drew a quick breath. There was a spotlight directly above, and the heat from it bore a hole in her head. Was the air conditioning even on? Goodness, he was just a man, and not even the most attractive one she'd ever met. Why the sudden discomfort?

"Is this your lovely wife, Captain?" The lady across from them asked.

Captain? Wife? Vanessa turned to the man, noting for the first time the white stripes on his sleeves. "I'm sorry, I didn't realize you were the captain." Her cheeks heated at the mistake. She was seated to the captain's right, without a doubt arranged by Grandfather.

He cleared his throat. "She is lovely but no, not my wife." He shrugged in a self-deprecating manner, and the other passengers at the table chuckled lightly.

He turned to her. "I'm Captain Romano, Miss Clark." He then addressed the other passengers who shared their table. "Allow me to introduce Miss Clark, from the United States of America." He started at his left and went around the table. "Dr. and Mrs. Whitehead, from the UK; Mr. and Mrs. Grantham, also from the UK; and Mr. and Mrs. Grosse, from Germany."

Vanessa nodded and smiled politely at them before they returned to their meals.

Miss Clark, I apologize for the blunder," one of the English ladies said. "But there was an empty chair next to the captain and he seemed to have been waiting for you." She looked between Vanessa and Captain Romano. "And you two make such a striking couple."

Vanessa's cheeks reddened, the curse of a light complexion, courtesy of Dad's Scandinavian ancestry.

"I haven't had the pleasure of meeting Miss Clark until now," the captain said.

Vanessa nodded. "Yes, what he said." She cringed inside. Why couldn't she come up with an appropriate reply when she needed one?

She busied herself with the perfectly seasoned potatoes on her plate instead. If she nodded and looked interested in the conversations around her, maybe she wouldn't have to say too much and could save herself from any more embarrassing responses.

"What state are you from, Miss Clark?" the German man asked, his accent evidence of his origins.

Vanessa paused to look at him. "I'm from Kansas."

His forehead wrinkled and he looked at his wife who gave him a small shrug.

"It's in the middle of the country. You know, lots of farming and fields, *The Wizard of Oz* and tornadoes," she explained, her words running together.

They nodded in understanding. Maybe she should stop talking now.

Vanessa waited for more questions, but thankfully none came, and she slowly let out a small breath of relief as the attention shifted from her.

One of the English men put his fork down. "Captain Romano, is Chef Teresa still on your crew?"

The captain smiled. "She certainly is. In fact, I have the same exact crew as last year." The pride in his voice was unmistakable.

Was this a common occurrence, to ask after the crew? Her knowledge of cruise etiquette was ridiculously poor despite what she'd read before coming, and even though Grandfather owned the vessel.

The questions continued for the rest of the meal, keeping the captain busy as he gave everyone his attention. How did he find the time to eat? His patience was admirable.

As the courses changed, the captain picked up the bottle of red wine, and Vanessa watched him pour a glass of the burgundy liquid for her. She thanked him and brought the glass to her lips, tasting a drop too small to swallow. The flavor was foreign to her, and she chased it down with a large gulp of the mineral water from the other tall glass in front of her. As she set the glass down, her hand trembled, and she tightened her grip on the stem until the base touched the table. How much longer until she could take refuge in her cabin?

As another waiter slipped a plate with the next course in front of her, she looked casually to the neighboring tables.

Couples. All the passengers sitting in the dining room were couples. Middle-aged and senior couples eating and talking and laughing. She couldn't find another person close to her age among the hundred and thirty passengers. The growing uneasiness tightened in her chest, and she suppressed a sigh. What had Grandfather done, sticking her on a fancy river cruise with the upper crust of Europe?

Captain Romano leaned in her direction. "Is everything all right, Miss Clark?"

Vanessa's tongue stuck to her palate, and she took another drink of the barely cold water. "Please, call me Vanessa, Captain." She raised her eyes to him. "Have you met my grandfather?"

One of the waiters came to the captain and handed him a small card. He tucked it in his pocket and then turned to the rest of the table. "Excuse me, ladies and gentlemen. I am needed elsewhere for a moment."

As he stood, he made eye contact with Vanessa. "Excuse me, Miss Clark," he said to her.

Vanessa nodded in response, not knowing what else to say. Why did he single her out?

What an unfortunate time for him to leave, and how disappointing for her. Now she'd have to wait for another chance to ask him about Grandfather.

Matias Romano looked around for the cruise director. When he spotted her across the room chatting with a group of passengers, he rose and excused himself from the last table. He always took the time to greet all the passengers after dinner and he wouldn't start making exceptions on this trip. But he could leave the rest of the evening in Anabela Rialto's capable hands. Mingling and interacting with the passengers were some of her duties, and Matias had observed over the last few trips and she seemed to enjoy that part of her job.

He had other matters to think about. Like Miss Vanessa Clark. They hadn't had a chance to talk in private at the table, and she had left the dining room abruptly after the dessert course was cleared, not even waiting for the after-dinner espresso to be served. If she had returned to her cabin, he'd have to talk to her some other time. But leaving her question unanswered wasn't ideal, and he felt obligated to set a friendly tone between them.

He quickly exited through the main lobby and climbed the stairs to the sun deck. He stopped short before reaching the bridge. There she was, to the starboard side, leaning casually by the railing, looking out to the city on the other side of the river. Her face was in profile, and her long blonde hair blew gently in the breeze. It was a lovely scene and she was a lovely woman, but there was nothing more to it.

So what if he was partial to blondes? A pretty face didn't hold much interest for him when she'd behaved so snobbishly at dinner. She had picked at her food and barely spoken to any of the other passengers, gazing around the room with an air of aloofness instead. As the only granddaughter of the company's president, she was probably used to the royal treatment, but that didn't give her the right to look down on the other passengers. Suddenly, talking to her wasn't a pressing matter anymore.

Why had he agreed to António Valadares's hare-brained idea? Sure, he could hardly deny any request from the president of the entire fleet of river cruise ships, but acting as a personal guide to his heiress granddaughter was not in Matias's job description. He should have said no, plain and simple. He was the captain, not a babysitter to a young woman who had everything. But his sense of duty had prevailed instead, as it usually did. There was more at stake than his personal preferences. Senhor Valadares had hinted at a problem with the future of the company, but Matias wasn't sure how it tied to the granddaughter.

Matias slowed down and squared his shoulders, letting out a slow breath. A hint of anticipation flared up, and he quickly squelched it, annoyed with himself at the twinge of attraction that sparked for a second too long. He only needed to talk to her. Nothing more.

She stood barefoot, her high-heeled sandals lying on their sides, her small purse next to them. Matias resisted the urge to return them to her and shoved his hands in his pants' pockets. He cleared his throat to greet her, but she spoke first.

"How many times have you made this trip, Captain?"

"Quite a few, Miss Clark." He faced the city as she did.

This was his seventeenth time up the river on this particular route. He knew because he'd been recording all his trips—not only the cruises but also the fishing and stocking ones—since he'd boarded his first boat as a deck hand at the age of fourteen. There were official records as well but he didn't like admitting to that level of precision and mostly kept the exact number to himself. "Miss Clark—"

She interrupted him. "And just how long have you been working for this company?"

Matias turned to her. "Is there a reason to your questioning, Miss Clark?" He kept his tone level and even, but his fingers tightened around the key ring inside his right pocket. What was it about this woman? He'd barely met her, and already she set him on edge in a way no one else had in his recent memory.

She leaned away from the railing and turned partially to him. "Just trying to determine how well you know my grandfather."

"Yes, you asked me that earlier. I'm sorry I didn't reply." They'd been interrupted by another passenger needing help, as he was so often during meals.

Matias took a quick breath and braced himself for more questions. He didn't know what to expect from her and it made him uneasy. The reaction was new to him, but she was more than a simple passenger, and it would serve him well not to forget the connections she had. "I have met your grandfather on several occasions since I started working at the company."

She turned away from him and let out a long sigh. "Probably more times than I have." Her words came out quick and low, and maybe not intended for him to hear.

"Is there a problem?" He paused and made eye contact.

"Not a problem exactly." She looked away and drummed her fingers along the rail.

"Is there something you're not happy with, Miss Clark?" They hadn't even departed, and already she had complaints. Usually he left the passenger-related matters to his cruise director, but not this one. She was in his hands, whether he liked it or not. "I know you're probably used to more personal service, but if you give us a chance, you might be pleasantly surprised."

Miss Clark's eyebrows knit in a scowl, but she didn't comment right away. After a long moment, she asked, "Are all the cabins as large as mine?"

"Excuse me?"

"The cabin assigned to me. Is that the standard cabin size?" She fidgeted with a length of hair, and when his eyes turned to it, she dropped it and flicked it behind her back.

The gesture lasted only a few seconds, but he lost his train of thought as it latched onto the woman in front of him. Matias struggled to resume their strange conversation. "Actually," he shook his head. "Uh, no. Your cabin is one of two deluxe cabins on the ship. We refer to them as the grand cabins, and they're reserved for our VIP passengers."

It was her turn to shake her head. "He did it, didn't he? He put me in that cabin?"

This conversation was turning more bizarre each minute. "If there's a problem with your cabin, I'll ask Miss Rialto to look into it. She's our cruise director, and I'll introduce you if you haven't had the chance to meet her. Your grandfather requested you stay in that particular cabin since it's the largest and best on the ship, and I have an obligation—"

Her eyes went wide. "Obligation? Obligation to what?"

Not to what, to whom. Her, to be exact. Matias didn't reply.

"To me, isn't it? You were going to say you have an obligation to me, weren't you?"

Matias flinched at her words and the way she'd read his mind. He rubbed his forehead. "It's not like how you make it sound." He forced his eyes to her. "Yes, I have an obligation toward you but it's the obligation I have toward all the passengers on board as well as my crew. I am the captain, after all."

Her shoulders relaxed a fraction, and Matias pressed on. "Your grandfather only wanted to make sure you have the best experience on this trip and even you can't fault him for that." Matias knew from his own research that she was his only granddaughter.

"I'm sure he did." She shook her head lightly, and her shoulders slumped even more, as if something weighed on her. "I don't need a babysitter, Captain. In case you haven't noticed, I'm a grown woman."

He'd noticed all right. More than he wished to, but he wouldn't be telling her that.

"Did he tell you why he wanted me to take this trip?" she asked.

Matias fumbled to find a reply and she waved him off. "That's okay, I don't want to know what he said. There's enough drama as it is."

It was family drama and he should stay out it. Well, most of it. He was already involved.

After a moment, she straightened and met his eyes. "At what time does the boat leave tomorrow?"

"The ship departs after lunch." He emphasized the word to correct her. It certainly wasn't a boat. "There's a guided excursion in the morning."

She bent to pick up her shoes and tucked the purse under her arm. "What are the rules about leaving?"

"Any time the ship is docked, you can leave at your leisure. But if you don't make it back before departure, we can't hold it for you."

She nodded. "That's only fair."

As she walked past him, he cleared his throat. "Nobody will prevent you from leaving if that's what you wish to do, but I hope you'll consider staying, Miss Clark." He wanted her to stay, and not just because the company's president had asked him. Proving to her that the trip was one worth taking had become more important than he'd anticipated.

Before she reached the staircase, he called after her. "Miss Clark."

She stopped and looked over her shoulder.

"Please be careful when you come out on the sun deck." He looked down at her bare feet, and she followed his gaze. "Oftentimes the floor is wet and it's easy to slip. I wouldn't want you to get hurt."

She pivoted, raising her fingers in a mock salute. "Aye, aye, Captain."

CHAPTER TWO

*T*he sun wasn't up yet when Matias arrived at the bridge. He greeted his first mate and nodded at the deckhand. "Good morning."

"*Bom dia, Capitão,*" the young man replied.

"You know the rule, Pedro. English only." Matias enunciated the words slowly and clearly. The young man's English wasn't perfect, but it wouldn't get any better if he didn't use it more.

Pedro's cheeks heated. "Yes, Captain." He put down the tray with two coffee mugs and breakfast croissants, then left.

"You could go easy on him," Miguel said from his chair.

"I could, but then it would take him longer to learn the language." English was the official language for a good reason. With so many international passengers, it was easier to set the expectation that everyone speak one common language than trying to accommodate individual needs. The expectation fell onto the crew as well.

Matias looked out the window. A thick fog hid the river and the banks under its gray layers. Some of the passengers would be surprised, but he had seen fog occur at any time of the year, regardless of the warm temperatures the day before. It would dissipate as they traveled up the river, as it usually did. He reached for the day's newspaper.

Something gray and solid moved ahead on the prow and he squinted. "Who's that out there?"

Miguel looked up from his place at the small desk. "That would be the special passenger." He turned back to checking the weather predictions on the iPad.

Matias's forehead wrinkled as he tried to distinguish who the figure was.

"You know, the one you've been asked to keep an eye on." Miguel kept his head down, unusually tempering his normal curiosity.

"That's Miss Clark out there?" Matias whacked the newspaper against the nearest counter, his voice unable to hide the annoyance and surprise at seeing her outside his window this early in the morning.

He yanked at the door and walked outside the bridge, rounding the prow to where she stood. For a moment, he thought he'd find her perched on the railing, à-la-*Titanic*-movie, but she was firmly planted on deck and wearing appropriate shoes. He let out a breath, the relief filling his chest and putting a stop to the adrenaline that had shot through his system a minute earlier.

The woman was throwing off his balance, and he hadn't even left the dock. He hadn't slept well, thinking about her and their exchange of words the night before, unable to get her out of his mind. What was he going to do about her?

She glanced at him. "Good morning, Captain."

Her cheeks and nose were red, and the top of her jacket covered the bottom half of her face up to her bottom lip. The hood flopped over her forehead, effectively hiding her long blonde hair. She looked younger than her early twenties, more vulnerable and insecure. The contradiction to the extremely put-together woman he'd met last night was more than what he could deal with at the moment, and he pushed the curiosity away.

Matias nodded at her, then turned to the bridge and knocked at the glass to get Miguel's attention. He pointed at the coffee carafe, and Miguel poured a cup and met him halfway.

Matias touched her arm, and when she turned toward him, he held the cup in front of her until she took it.

She rested the cup against the railing and pulled the zipper down with her left hand to uncover her mouth. Then she sipped quietly, both hands wrapped around the mug, her eyes closed in soft appreciation.

"What are you doing out here at five o'clock in the morning, Miss Clark?"

"I wanted to see the sunrise, Captain Romano." Her breath came out in little puffs, and her voice held a small tremble.

"That's not going to happen today." His words sounded harsher than he intended and he cringed inside.

Miss Clark raised an eyebrow at him over the rim of the cup and kept sipping.

He softened his voice. "I mean, the sun will rise, of course, but we won't be able to see it through the fog." Before he lost the gumption, he continued. "Listen, Miss Clark. I wanted to apologize for my gruff words last night."

She lowered the cup and adjusted her fingers around it. "I do too, Captain." She kept her eyes down on the dark liquid for a moment, then raised them to him. "I mean, apologize. I was angry at my grandfather, and I shouldn't have taken it out on you."

Anger? There was more to the story between António Valadares and his granddaughter than what Matias knew, and he probably should keep it that way.

"And I shouldn't have reacted so poorly. I'm sorry." The tightness in his chest eased a bit as he voiced the apology. He always kept his behavior professional toward his passengers, and he would treat her the same way.

Miss Clark's expression relaxed, and her eyes locked on his. She was taller than most women he knew, and the short distance between them put her nearly to eye level with him. She had green eyes framed by long light-brown eyelashes, and a few freckles dotted her skin on the bridge of her nose. No make-up this morning. Just delicate, creamy skin and eyes the color of the river on a winter day.

For a moment, a prick of interest niggled at him. What was she like in her day-to-day life? What did she do for fun? And why was she on this trip when she obviously hadn't chosen to come?

He occasionally wondered about a passenger on a personal level, but only in passing and seldom with the intent to truly know more. But this situation was different. His questions went beyond superficial interest this time.

It didn't help that she was young and attractive, and it had been a long time since Matias had given himself permission to think about a woman and the possibility of going out on a date. Fortunately, he had enough responsibilities to keep him physically busy and emotionally unavailable.

If only his thoughts were as easy to direct.

Vanessa looked away from Captain Romano's chocolate-colored eyes.

What had just happened? Yesterday they'd been short and almost rude with each other, and now, after offering apologies, something had passed between them: something warm, zingy, and unexpected.

Something totally unrelated to the coffee in her hands.

He took a step back and she did the same. Good. More distance between them was what she needed. Standing near the broad-shouldered captain with the deep brown eyes and the sexy voice muddled her thoughts. She had to get away from him and clear her head.

Vanessa tipped the cup and drank the rest of the coffee the captain had brought her earlier, most likely from his own pot.

"Was this your coffee?" She held the cup to him and he took it.

"We keep a carafe well filled."

She slipped her hands into the kangaroo pocket of her jacket. "Thank you for sharing. I underestimated the weather this morning."

"You're welcome. And you're not the only passenger who didn't expect to see fog in the summer."

They stood in silence for a minute, watching the rolling wisps of gray as if they'd part to reveal the city on the other side. Vanessa peered at the captain, but, just like the fog that hid everything around them, his face disclosed nothing of his thoughts.

A tap sounded on the window, and they turned to see the other crewman motioning to the phone. Captain Romano nodded back at him.

"It looks like you're needed." Vanessa tipped her head toward the bridge.

"After you." He gestured for her to walk ahead of

him. "By the way, good choice on footwear."

Vanessa stood there for a moment as he entered the bridge, a faltering smile on her face at the unexpected comment.

When she arrived at her cabin, she fell back on the wide bed and kicked off her shoes. They weren't exactly traditional deck shoes but more of a crossbreed, with a ballerina-flat shape and solid rubber soles. No slipping on the sun deck in these babies. And they were red, which she loved.

Even better, Captain Romano approved of her choice. It shouldn't matter that he did, but the happy feeling inside her wouldn't abate, even when she tried to force it to go. After a short moment, she gave up the fight. When was the last time a man complimented her? Nothing came to mind. She'd had a few dates in college, but the compliments had seldom sounded sincere. Compared to the captain, those guys had only been overgrown boys who mostly wanted one thing from her. Captain Romano was older, but there was something about him that went beyond age and maturity: something intriguing and attractive.

She shook her head. It was pathetic. *She* was pathetic. A man had offered her a compliment and there she went setting him up as the yardstick of perfection by which all other males had to be measured. Had she been like this on campus? No wonder she'd gone out on only five dates in the four years she'd lived in Kansas City for her degree.

She pulled off her hoodie and sat cross-legged against the tufted headboard. Her cabin was immense and luxurious like everything else on the ship. The king bed was a guilty pleasure, too large for a single girl who wouldn't be sharing it with anyone else. She'd stretched in all directions the night before, not even coming close to the edge. Even the bathroom was built for a couple, with double shower heads, double vanities, double fluffy, ultra-white towels. Was she supposed to use both sets of towels or only one?

Outside the wide French doors, on a narrow balcony, two chairs flanked a small table. Maybe later, when the sun shone to the west, she'd sit outside and gaze at the city of Porto, putting her feet up on the second chair.

The memory of her bedroom in her tiny apartment back home sprang to mind, so much smaller than this cabin and certainly lacking all the amenities this one boasted. Everything she'd left in Kansas was clouded in uncertainty—a foreign feeling after living there all her life—and she still had a hard time reconciling the only reality she'd ever known with her new privileged circumstances.

But who wouldn't? She'd gone to bed one night counting her pennies for the rest of the month, and she'd woken up to find out she was a Portuguese heiress. If there was an easy way to adjust to that, no one had told her. The position didn't come with a manual. Furthermore, Dad hadn't wanted her to come and Grandfather now wanted her to stay. And she didn't know what she wanted.

Vanessa suppressed a laugh. Just a few weeks ago she'd been watching the sun set over the Kansas plains, as she'd done as long as she could remember. But that was a whole world away and harder and harder to remember with each day spent in Portugal.

All thanks to Grandfather who was responsible for the drastic change in her life. He actually saw himself as the hero who'd rescued her from her pitiful existence in Kansas. Yet, she couldn't bring herself to commend him for it or for anything else, not after all the anxiety and confusion he'd caused for the past weeks.

Like this trip he'd sent her on and the captain he'd asked to spy on her.

There she was, thinking of the captain again. Vanessa pulled out her phone. It was too early for breakfast, and she didn't want to call down to the kitchen, even if the crew thought of her as a VIP passenger. Such a strange situation to be in.

Vanessa pulled up the search engine on her smartphone and typed *Captain Romano* and *Princess Catarina*. The links and pictures came up immediately. She followed a link to Gold River Cruises, Grandfather's company, where Captain Matias Romano had been working for the past sixteen years, according to the information she read. Another page pointed to a small entry about the captain himself: Ernesto Matias da Silva Romano, age thirty-one, born in

Porto, Portugal. His parents were briefly mentioned, but there was nothing about a wife or children. He didn't wear a wedding ring, but that was hardly a reliable indication of his present marital status.

On the company's website, a picture of the *Princess Catarina* at the christening ceremony three years ago showed Captain Romano next to a striking woman who had long black hair and wore a red cocktail dress. Maybe he did have a wife after all and she was very selective about her public appearances.

Vanessa blew out a breath and put the phone to sleep. It didn't matter if the captain was married. That had nothing to do with his job and certainly less to do with her. Didn't Dad always say that too much interest was almost as bad as too little expectation? Vanessa had learned the hard way, expecting as much of others as she did of herself. The disappointment was hard to take at times. She hadn't learned to curb her curiosity either.

The phone rattled against the surface of the bedside table. Vanessa swiped at the screen and groaned when Dad's number showed up. She hesitated for a second before accepting the call.

"Vanessa. About time," Dad said by way of greeting.

She sat on the bed. "Hi, Dad, how are you?"

"I've been calling you and leaving messages, and you didn't answer."

Even after she'd left for college, Dad had a hard time letting go of checking on her. "I'm answering now, Dad. I was busy last night at the captain's dinner."

"A fancy dinner, I bet." He paused for a deep breath. "What's the ship like?"

"It's very nice." Vanessa held back a sigh of her own, leaned against the headboard, and settled in for a longer conversation than she wanted. "You'd like it, Dad. The woodwork is impressive." She spent the next ten minutes answering his reluctant questions. He was curious, but didn't want to show it. Vanessa described the details she knew he'd be interested in, but not so much as to make it obvious. Her being away on this trip and aboard the ship was already hard enough on him.

She closed her eyes after hanging up. Usually, he called her only every few days, but his calls had become more frequent since she'd arrived in Portugal. Which was unfortunate because Dad's earnestness could only be taken in small doses.

After a quick shower, she changed into her favorite pair of dark skinny jeans and added a thin cardigan over a gauzy top and chunky necklace. She pulled her hair into a low ponytail and applied some light make-up. It was only breakfast, and dressy casual was probably fine.

In truth, the dress code caused her some anxiety. Before the trip, Vanessa had read blogs on river cruises and social procedures aboard five-star ships. Despite her reluctance, being prepared made more sense. Her lack of knowledge would probably appall some of her fellow passengers but, at this point, Vanessa could only hope they wouldn't see right through her inexperience.

What about the captain? Did he know this was her first time on a cruise? How much had Grandfather told him?

She glanced at the full-size mirror behind the door one last time. Much better than this morning when she'd seen the captain near the bridge. The key-card went in the front pocket of her jeans.

She was ready to face the day...and Captain Romano.

Find *Meet Me At Sunrise* on Amazon

ACKNOWLEDGMENTS

Sometimes you plan a story for years and sometimes a story springs on you in a short few weeks.

Knox and Jacinta were such a fun surprise!

Thank you to my critique partners (Laura, Lori, and Sally) for the almost-everyday support and brainstorming.

A big thank you to my fabulous editors, Michele and Ellie, who not only helped me turn my story into something much better, but were also super-quick about it.

Again, my thanks go to my mother for taking me to Porto again on my last trip to Portugal. As many times as I'd been there, I hadn't crossed the Dom Luís bridge before, and I'm glad I did. It gave me the inspiration for a great scene between Knox and Jacinta.

This is a short little story but it was so much fun to write and I love how it turned out. I hope all of you will fall in love with Knox and Jacinta as well.

Thank you!

THE AUTHOR

𝓛ucinda Whitney was born and raised in Portugal, where she received a Master's degree from the University of Minho in Braga, in Portuguese/English teaching.

She lives in northern Utah with her husband and four children. When she's not reading and writing, she can be found with a pair of knitting needles, or tending her herb garden.

She's the author of The Secret Life of Daydreams and One Small Chance, her LDS romance series named A Love Story from Portugal. *Hold Me At Twilight* is the first book in the new Romano Family series.

Please visit her website at lucindawhitney.com for more information and news.

Printed in Great Britain
by Amazon

56925403R00066